Chickosaurus Rex

PAM HARVEY

Illustrated by Greg Gaul

The Story Characters

John Angus Alex

The Story Setting

TABLE OF CONTENTS

Dad and His Mirrors

My dad is an antique dealer. He goes around looking at pieces of old furniture. When he finds things he wants, he buys them inexpensively. Then he fixes them up and sells them.

Dad specializes in mirrors. His workshop at the back of our house has one whole wall of mirrors. Dad fixes up all of the mirrors back there.

Some need frames, some are cracked. Some need more black stuff on their backs. And Dad loves them all.

He polishes them with Mom's old dish towels. I think that he even talks to the mirrors as he polishes them!

I hate those mirrors. They're why I've got Bart instead of a 90-pound dog. (I wanted a dog that bares its teeth and makes your hair stand on end!)

“Bart is clean and neat, and he won’t wet the legs of my antique tables. You know what I mean,” said Dad.

He said this when I whined that other kids didn’t have a chicken for a pet.

At least Bart isn't an ordinary chicken. He's a silky bantam. Silky bantams look like they've got ragged cotton balls stuck all over them. Their heads look like one big cotton ball!

Their head feathers shoot out over their faces. Silky bantam roosters have a screeching, loud COCKADOODLEDOOO. But somehow it's not very scary when it comes out of a bird hardly bigger than a pigeon.

CHAPTER 2

Bluffing!

Last Monday at school, we were talking about our pets.

"Arnold is my rottweiler. He's been known to munch cats by the dozen," said Angus McLean. (Angus looks like he eats whole cows for dinner!)

“I’ve got a python called Sly,” said Alex Browning, rubbing his football hands together. “He eats live rats.”

"I keep 27 bad-tempered spiders in an old fish tank in my bedroom," said John Vega.

We all shuddered a little at that one

Then Angus said to me, "What sort of pet have you got at home, Flake?"

They call me "Flake" because once, only once, I had a speck of dandruff on my sweater. That speck might not even have been mine. But I've been stuck with Flake ever since.

And if you're called Flake, you aren't going to admit to owning a fluffy, white chicken!

"I've got a chickosaurus rex," I said.

Angus eyeballed me. "A what?"

“A chickosaurus rex! It’s a meat-eating bird.” I shrugged, acting really cool. “Dad found it when he was looking for antiques. Its owner had died. Dad was buying some old furniture when he saw this huge bird in a cage.”

"Of course, he didn't know it was a chickosaurus rex, or he wouldn't have brought it home." I sighed, trying to look as if it was too much to talk about. "He didn't realize that it ate terriers."

“Get out of here!” said Angus, crossing his arms over his chest. “You’re bluffing, Flake.”

I looked Angus straight in the eyes. “It’s absolutely true,” I said.

"Didn't I tell you about the time it got out of its cage? It flew over the fence and ate Mrs. Jeffers's terrier. When it flew back, it kept spitting balls of fur all over the lawn. That's how I caught it. It was choking on a big fur ball, and I pushed it back into its cage."

Everyone was laughing, but they weren't quite sure. They were trying to figure out if I was making it all up. John was even looking a bit sick. (His mother owned a terrier.)

Angus was still standing with his arms crossed. “How come we haven’t heard about this bird before?” he asked.

"You never asked before," I said. I yawned as if I was really bored.

"Well, I'd like to see it."

I almost choked in the middle of my yawn. "You idiot!" I said to myself. Of course they'd want to see it.

I thought very fast. “It always spits on strangers.”

Angus shrugged.

“And some books say that its saliva is a type of acid,” I said.

Angus shrugged again.

"And it makes the most terrible noise. It can make you deaf with just one cry. We wear earmuffs around the house just in case it squawks."

Angus bent down to where I was sitting. His breath smelled of tuna fish. “I’m coming over tonight to see this chickorexaty. And so are the rest of us. Right, everyone?”

Everyone grinned and nodded.

I gulped. "It's not a chickorexaty It's a chickosaurus rex," I managed to whisper.

"See you at five o'clock." They all walked off, leaving me feeling really stupid. What was I going to do now?

Plan C

I thought of three plans:

A. Become ill during math, so they'd have to cart me off to the hospital. (Would Mr. James believe me?)

B. Fake a robbery at our place (How could I do that?)

C. Stick pretend fangs on Bart to make him look scary.

Plan C was the only one I could try.

Angus waved to me at the gate. "See you at five o'clock," he shouted.

He had to shout because dark thunder clouds were rolling across the sky. And the booms of thunder could drown out even Angus's loud mouth!

I ran home. I got there just as an icy rain started coming down. There was a note on the table from Mom.

It said, “Dad and I have gone to the store. Help yourself to a snack.”

"Great," I muttered. Now I couldn't get Mom to call Angus's mom to say that I was sick. (Plan D was that I had come down with an infectious disease. I'd thought of it on the way home.)

It looked like I had to stick with the false-fang plan. First, I cut triangles out of old butter containers. Next, I put pieces of sticky tape on them.

Then I went down the stairs and through Dad's workshop. I opened the doors to look for Bart.

"Bart! Food! Here, Bart, Bart, Bart!"

He wasn't anywhere.

I looked at my watch. It was almost five o'clock.

"Bart!" I yelled. "Cracked corn, Bart! Cracked corn!" Bart loved cracked corn, but he didn't appear.

I went back inside. I was thinking fast. I needed to make up a story about how my chickosaurus rex had escaped.

Maybe I should take the frozen lamb out of the freezer. I could cover it with Mom's old feather scarf and place it in the road. A roadkill-chickosaurus rex!

CHAPTER 4

Where Is It?

I made a move toward the freezer, but there was a knock at the door.

It was followed quickly by another knock. Then another. Three knocks—Angus, John, and Alex. I gulped. Perhaps I could hide under a table?

"Hey, Flake! I see you. Let us in!"

Angus was tall enough to see through the pane of frosted glass in the door. Angus would've also seen the empty driveway. So he knew there was no one else here to save me.

I opened the door, and they crowded into the hall. I tried to look cool. "Do you want a snack? Do you want to play on my computer? I just got a new game." (This wasn't true, but they wouldn't know.)

John looked interested, but Angus shook his head. "We've come to see the chicko-whatsit."

"It's a chickosaurus rex," I mumbled.

I was just about to explain that it had been missing all day. Suddenly, a screeching squawk sounded out back.

I took no notice, except to mutter, "Oh, he's back."

But the others jumped.

"What was that?" whispered Alex.

"It sounded pretty mean," said John.

The squawk came again—a fierce, ear-splitting howl. Bart must have heard what I said about the cracked corn. He was on the prowl.

"Is that your bird? I want to see it now!" said Angus, a glint in his eye.

"Well," I began, "now's not really a good time."

Angus elbowed me out of the way and headed toward Dad's workshop. I had no other option but to follow him.

The Chickosaurus Rex

Outside, the storm was beginning again, and storm clouds darkened the sky. When we reached the workshop, it was pretty dark.

I switched on Dad's reading lamp. The light reflected off the mirrors. It made everything brighter than daylight.

There was Bart. He was standing in the doorway, as wet as a fish. His feathers were standing up like spikes. He looked as if he had on some sort of terrible helmet.

"Well, guys," I said sheepishly, "there's my chickosaurus rex."

There was a mighty scream from John. He took off as though he'd been bitten by one of his spiders. Then Alex started making gurgling noises in his throat. He backed out of the workshop.

I glanced at Angus and was amazed by the look on his face. He was as white as Mom's tennis socks, and his bottom lip was trembling.

Bart gave another howl. I turned around to tell him to knock it off, when Angus bolted after the others. In less than a second, there were three sets of feet running down the driveway!

I couldn't move. What was going on? Surely they weren't scared of a little, wet bantam calling out for his dinner? Hadn't they ever seen a chicken before?

I stepped forward to get Bart in from the rain. Then suddenly I saw it.

Reflected in Dad's mirrors, Bart was a six-foot-tall, spiky-feathered, war-helmeted, bloodcurdle-screaming, hungry chickosaurus rex!

At school these days, we never talk about our pets. And no one calls me Flake anymore!

At home, I don't complain anymore about Dad's mirrors. And I don't whine that I haven't got a dog. Sometimes I even help Dad polish the mirrors. And he can't understand why that makes me giggle.

And Bart isn't "Bart" anymore—that's not a name for a chickosaurus rex! Now I call him Warrior.

I've also started to teach Bart about terriers, just in case the boys ever decide to visit again!

GLOSSARY

antique
furniture or art from an earlier time

bluffing
pretending, making it up

dandruff
flakes of dry scalp

eyeballed
looked closely at

infectious

easily caught from germs

option

choice

reflected

showed an image

rottweiler

a very large breed of dog

specializes

is an expert in

Talking with the Author and Illustrator

Pam Harvey (author)

What is your favorite thing?

A silver bracelet that is made out of two spoons welded together.

What do you like about yourself?

The way I smile a lot.

What is your favorite midnight snack?

Dried fruit, so I don't wake up everyone.

Greg Gaul (illustrator)

What is your favorite thing?

My family and my friends.

What do you like about yourself?

I like telling bad jokes.

Why did the cow jump over the moon?

To get to the udder side.

sundance™

Published by Sundance Publishing
33 Boston Post Road West, Suite 440, Marlborough, MA 01752
800-343-8204

First published 1999 as Sparklers by
Blake Education, Locked Bag 2022, Glebe 2037, Australia
Exclusive United States Distribution: Sundance Publishing

ISBN 978-0-7608-8103-3

Printed by Nordica International Ltd.
Manufactured in Guangzhou, China
May, 2010
Nordica Job#: 05-53-10
Sundance/Newbridge PO#: 225991